The Magical Hike

The Power of Nature

Created by
Alexandra Angheluta

Illustrated by
Polina Hrytskova

Once upon a time there was a girl named Pearl.
She rarely went outside to play and explore.

Pearl had quite a problem.
Where she lived, it rained in winter, spring, summer and autumn.
Therefore, Pearl decided to spend most of her time at home.

One day, Pearl shared with her mom,
"I feel disconnected being inside all alone.
But I don't feel close to anything that is not a part of our home."

Her mom handed her a raincoat, and a pair of shoes.
She told Pearl, "Go for a hike and see some views."

Pearl asked her to change her decision,
But her mom assured her that there would be no revision.
She then looked up at the sky and said,

"I promise you, these clouds will shift on by.
You will then see the true color of the sky."

Pearl's mom continued, "First, close your eyes.
In the barn there is a surprise!"
She asked Pearl to reach out her hand.
And when Pearl opened her eyes, she gazed at an owl so grand!

With eyes so big and feathers noticeably white,
Pearl knew she had a guide home, should she lose sight.
The owl could observe what others could not,
It would be there for Pearl if she felt distraught.

With the owl on her shoulder she set off to wander,
But the thought, "Why can't I stay home?" was all she could ponder.

Pearl had found herself among some trees.
To her surprise, she felt lighthearted and free.
With every step she took she felt a bit warmer,
Pearl knew this natural heat was making her stronger.

On her magical hike, she observed so much.
Surrounded by nature, she felt deeply in touch.
And even though she was all alone,
She'd never felt this connected, like here in the unknown.

With every sight she saw outside,
She discovered a new part of herself, inside.
She heard a voice come from within,
And the things that voice said made her grin.

"Just like a waterfall, I am powerful and pouring with emotion."

And just like a river, I am constantly flowing.
There may be rocks in my path,
but I am fluid and I always find a way around."

"Just like a lake, I am peaceful and calm."

"I need time to sit and be still. I need moments of silence to understand the quieter parts of me. Just like stacked rocks, I too can find a soothing balance."

"Just like a volcano, I become destructive at times."

"And just like me, the earth heals and regrows.
The earth replants itself over time, and so can I."

"Just like the roots of a tree, I too must stay grounded. With my roots planted deep, I am sturdy enough to reach the sky."

"I am a flower that has beautiful strength, just like the flowers that sprout through dirt."

"Just like a cave, there are hidden parts of myself that I must journey through, even when there is no glimmer of light to be seen."

"And just like me, the earth has dark and vast spaces that are yet to be discovered."

"Just like clouds, I fill up with emotion.
I sometimes feel dark, heavy and gray.

And just like rain, I cry too.
I let go, and then I am as light as a feather again.

And when my tears dry, I see the flowers they grew."

Just like the blue sky, I am always in existence. Even when I feel clouded, I know my bright color is still within reach. I am like a clear sky waiting to be seen after a foggy morning."

Just like air, I am a part of everything. Sometimes I cannot see something. Sometimes I can only feel it. Just like wind."

"Just like the ocean, I am full of life.
And if I dive deep, I may find treasure. I may find myself."

"I am a special and precious gem. Just like a pearl."

The magical hike helped Pearl see things differently than before.
With a clear path leading home, the owl knew it was free to soar.

Pearl ran up to her mom and said, "Mom, even though we have a house I think the Earth is our home. And even though you take care of me, I think the Earth takes care of us all. And mom, the Earth talks to us. We just have to listen."

Her mom smiled brightly and responded, "I think you're right!"

Pearl now spends her time outside, rain or shine.
She sits down and sees with a new set of eyes.

She hears herself whisper: "I am never alone.
We are all connected. We all live here together on Earth."

How much the owl helped with the wisdom Pearl gained,
Nobody knows for sure, but the fact remains the same:

Nature is magic. And so are you.

"If you want the rainbow,
you gotta put up with the rain.

- Dolly Parton

Nature Affirmations

- I am special and precious like a pearl.
- I am deep like an ocean.
- I flow like a river.
- I am as peaceful as a lake.
- I am as powerful as a waterfall.
- I am fluid like water.
- I am grounded and supported by the earth.
- I can reach new heights like the branches of a tree.
- Nature helps me flourish.
- The sun will rise again tomorrow, so will I. Every day is a new day.
- I am a part of nature, therefore I am beautiful.
- I let go freely, like the leaves in autumn.
- I take risks to soar, just like a bird.
- No matter what storms are passing, I am the blue sky.
- A seed will sprout into a plant when it is ready. I give myself time.
- I have different phases of growth, just like a butterfly.

About the Author

Using the magic of play and imagination, Alexandra has been connecting with children for more than a decade! With an educational background in social work and play therapy, she felt inspired to create stories to help children heal and grow. Alexandra is the creator of the Magical Affirmations series! All of the books focus on healing from within by using the power of thoughts and words. The books focus on emotional growth topics such as self-love, faith, courage, connection, and inner light.

She is a believer that play, imagination, and words of affirmation have the ability to transform. Alexandra now spends her time in Portland Oregon playing with children, writing in nature and connecting to spirit on the yoga mat. You can follow Alexandra on Instagram @magical_affirmations or alexandra_angheluta22.

Look for these other titles:

- The Magical Globes: The Power of Having Faith
- The Magical Mind: The Power of Your Thoughts
- The Magical Dreamcatcher: The Power of Believing in Your Inner Light
- The Magical Gray Flower: The Power of Self-Love

This book is dedicated to us all.

May we take care of Earth and be guided through all of her magical ways.

Printed in the United States of America First Printing: 2021
ISBN: 9798731972840
Library of Congress Control Number: 2021907008

Independently published by PlaySitters Hawaii

Made in United States
Troutdale, OR
12/05/2024

25948886R00021